I0692720

BY
LADORRIS
THOMAS
No bullying allowed!
Don't Be a Bully,
Be a Blessing

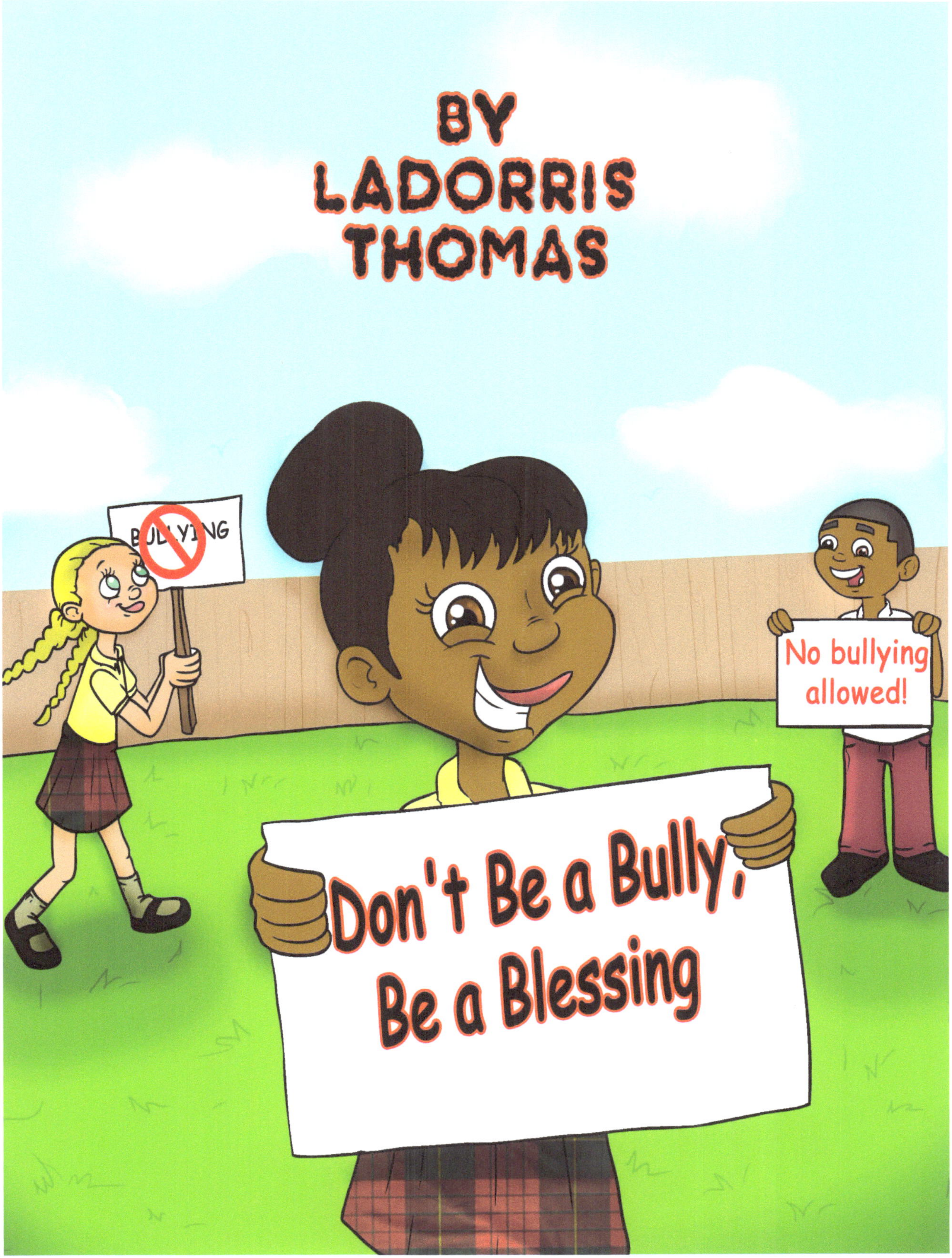

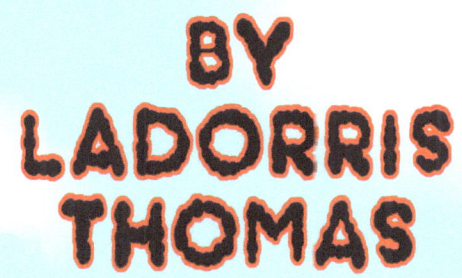

*Don't Be a Bully, Be a Blessing*

Published by Lifelong Blessing, LLC
Edited and Designed by Rachel McDermott
Cover Design and Illustrations by Jasmine Mills

Published in the United States of America
ISBN 13: 978-0692646724
ISBN 10: 0692646728

1. Fiction
2. Children

References
http://www.merriam-webster.com/dictionary/bully
http://www.merriam-webster.com/dictionary/blessing
http://www.merriam-webster.com/dictionary/jealous

Contact LaDorris:
P.O. Box 742666
Riverdale, GA 30274

thelifedigger.com

# Dedication

This book is dedicated to all of the little boys and girls whose lives are affected by bullies. I want them to know that it is never their fault when someone bullies them. They should be able to tell an adult when someone is bullying or being mean to them. And they should always know that they are loved and very important.

# Introduction

Lydia is seven years old, and she is in 2nd grade at a new school. She was named after her grandma Dia. Lydia enjoys her new school until a few girls start bullying her. This makes Lydia sad, and she always wears a frown. She gets really bad tummy aches when she goes to school because she is afraid of the bullies, but she doesn't tell her grandma or teacher about what is going on. One day, Lydia unexpectedly meets a new friend who helps her face her fears.

# Vocabulary Words

**What does bully mean?**

To frighten, hurt, or threaten (a smaller or weaker person)

**What is a blessing?**

Something that makes a person happy or content

"Lydia! It's time for school. Come on, get dressed so you don't miss the bus," calls Grandma from downstairs.

"I wish we had a car so Grandma could pick me up from school," Lydia says to herself.

"Mr. Stewart will not wait for you. Let's go to the bus stop. We only have three minutes!" says Grandma.

"Okay, Grandma! I'm coming!" Lydia tells her grandma.

As Lydia gets out of bed, she says, "I'm tired! I just want to go back to bed. I don't want to go to school today. Or ever. I wish school was cancelled forever! I wish! I wish! I wish!"

All of a sudden, an angel appears! "Did somebody make a wish?" she asks.

Lydia is surprised, and she screams.

"Lydia? What's wrong?" asks Grandma.

"Shhhh," says the angel. "It's okay! I won't hurt you. My name is Angel, and I am your friend. I've come to help you!"

"Lydia, what's the matter?" asks Grandma.

"Uh, nothing, Grandma!" says Lydia.

"Well, hurry! I can see the bus."

The angel disappears, and Lydia says, "Coming, Gram!"

After the school bus arrives, Lydia climbs the steps and sits three seats behind the driver. She doesn't like school and wishes she could just stay at home with her grandma. She also wishes she had an older sibling to protect her from the school bullies.

"Hey, Lydia! I know you heard me say hello," says Tina, one of the bullies. She is sitting a few seats behind Lydia.

"I wish they would just disappear already!" whispers Lydia to herself.

The angel appears in the seat next to Lydia. "You're making wishes again?" she asks.

"Huh? It's you again! Where did you come from?" asks Lydia.

"Shhh! You're the only one that can see me. I can't tell you where I came from. Just know someone sent me to help you."

"How are you going to help me? Can you fight? Those girls are tough." Lydia sighs. "If only I knew how to fight."

"Lydia, fighting isn't the only way to beat a bully," says Angel. "When you have confidence, you will be able to stand up to them. Confidence is believing in yourself."

"Believing in myself? What do I have to believe in? They call me names, they pull my hair, and they tell the boys not to talk to me."

"Well, I've been watching you. You're very smart and well-mannered, you're a great artist, and you're a joy to your grandmother," says Angel.

"How have you been watching me?" asks Lydia.

"I know someone who has eyes everywhere," says Angel.

"Eyes everywhere? Well, can you ask your friend that has a lot of eyes to see if Grandma will let me stay home tomorrow? And when these bullies will leave me alone?"

"Oh, so now you're talking to yourself?" asks Ariel, another bully. She is sitting across the aisle from Tina.

Tina says, "You're so weird, Ly-dodo!" Both she and Ariel start laughing at Lydia.

Lydia sees that Angel has disappeared. She tries to ignore the girls because she thinks it will make them leave her alone. She has been bullied by these girls since she started coming to this school, but none of the adults know because she's too afraid to tell.

After arriving at school, Lydia skips breakfast and sits outside the classroom.

"I wish I could have stayed home today," Lydia whispers to herself.

"I'm going to call you the wishing princess," says Angel.

"Oh no! Not you again!" says Lydia.

"Why are you sitting alone?"

"I'm avoiding the bullies. They like to sit inside and talk before class."

"Did you know that most bullies are jealous of others?" asks Angel.

"What is that supposed to mean?" asks Lydia.

"Jealous means feeling anger toward someone because he or she is more successful," says Angel.

"So they bully me because I'm smart, creative, and others like me?"

"Exactly! Many bullies don't like themselves. They bully others so they will feel better," says Angel.

"Oh. I guess that makes sense."

"And did you know that most bullies have been bullied before?"

"Then why are they so mean if they know how it feels?"

"They think being mean is the only way to make others like them."

"I just don't understand," says Lydia. "I wish I was home watching *Gullah Gullah Island* and *Arthur*."

When class starts, Angel disappears and Lydia goes back inside.

Ms. Humphries enters the room. "Good morning, class!"

The students say, "Good Morning, Ms. Humphries!"

"Today we will do an activity called stand and tell," says Ms. Humphries. "When it's your turn, stand and tell us your name and one thing you're good at."

When it is Lydia's turn, she stands and says, "My named is Lydia, and I'm creative."

Ariel says, "You mean Ly-dodo!"

All of the kids burst into laughter, and Lydia hangs her head. Ms. Humphries tells them to quiet down.

"That is very nice, Lydia," says Ms. Humphries.

"Thank you," whispers Lydia.

Lydia slowly walks back to her seat. She is too sad to pay attention to what the other students say about themselves.

After the morning activity, it is time for recess. Lydia sits by herself, as usual.

"I really wish I didn't have to come to school!" Lydia says.

"I'm going to call you the wish girl," says Angel. "You have more wishes than a wishing well."

"It's you again!" says Lydia. "I can't talk to you. The bullies think I'm talking to myself."

"Lydia, I know you're only in second grade, but you shouldn't worry about what other people think."

"Why?"

"Did you know that worrying can lead to stomach problems?" Angel asks.

"Is that why my stomach hurts when I'm at school?" asks Lydia.

"Yes. You're supposed to come to school to learn, have fun, and grow!"

"But how can I have fun without friends?"

"You don't need friends to have fun," says Angel.

"Well, then how do I have fun by myself?" asks Lydia.

"There are lots of ways to have fun by yourself. For starters, you can play hopscotch."

"But I don't know how to play hopscotch."

"Come on! I'll show you how," says Angel.

"All right." Lydia follows Angel to the hopscotch squares marked on the pavement.

"Now hop on these squares and repeat after me," says Angel.

Lydia gets ready. "Okay, what do I say?"

"My name is Lydia and I'm the best! My name is Lydia and I am blessed! My name is Lydia and I love myself!"

"I can't say that. They'll laugh at me!" says Lydia.

"Don't ever say you can't!" says Angel. "Come on, repeat after me while you hopscotch!"

"Okay," says Lydia.

As Lydia plays hopscotch, she repeats after Angel. "My name is Lydia and I'm the best! My name is Lydia and I am blessed! My name is Lydia and I love myself!"

"Every time someone bullies you, say this chant out loud," Angel says.

"Okay, I will," says Lydia.

After a while, Tina walks up to Lydia. "Are you talking to yourself again, Ly-dodo?"

Lydia looks at her and says, "My name is Lydia and I'm the best! My name is Lydia and I am blessed! My name is Lydia and I love myself!"

Tina pushes Lydia, but Lydia does not fight back.

"Fighting is not the only way to beat a bully," says Lydia.

Tina looks surprised. "What's that supposed to mean!"

"It means that I don't have to say or do hurtful things to you, even if you hurt me. My name is Lydia and I'm the best! My name is Lydia and I am blessed! My name is Lydia and I love myself!"

Tina finally left Lydia alone.

Lydia felt really good as she continued to play hopscotch. She beat a bully without getting into a fight! Angel's chant really worked.

The chant became Lydia's favorite saying. Whenever someone was mean to her, she would yell, "My name is Lydia and I'm the best! My name is Lydia and I am blessed! My name is Lydia and I love myself!"

Lydia began to gain confidence, and she soon became a blessing to some of her classmates. They would yell the chant using their names when bullies said mean things to them, and eventually the bullies walked away.

These kids were glad that Lydia taught them the chant, and they became friends with her.

Lydia soon realizes that school can be fun. She looks forward to going every day.

One night a few weeks later, Lydia is excited as she goes to bed. She drew a nice picture, and she will show it to her class in the morning for Show and Tell.

"That is a lovely picture, sweetheart," says Grandma when she comes to say goodnight.

"Thank you, Gram! I can't wait to show my friends at school," says Lydia.

"I'm glad you are excited to go to school. I knew you would settle in."

"Actually, I used to be afraid of school," says Lydia. "There were some bullies in my class. But they aren't bothering me anymore."

"Why didn't you tell me? I could have helped you," says Grandma.

"I didn't know what to say. I thought it was my fault," says Lydia.

"What changed?"

"I learned to believe in myself," says Lydia, "and that helped me stand up to the bullies. It also helped some of the other kids, and they are my friends now."

"Well, that's wonderful. I am so proud of you. But I want you to remember something. You can always talk to me about anything. You are very important to me, and I love you." Grandma gives Lydia a hug.

"Yes, Grandma. I love you, too!" says Lydia.

"Goodnight," says Grandma.

After Grandma leaves the room, Angel appears one last time.

"Lydia, what your grandmother said is important," says Angel. "You should always talk to her or another trusted adult, like your teacher, if you are having problems."

"Yes, I know that now," says Lydia.

"Also, school is your practice for the real world. How you handle problems at school is how you will handle problems when you grow up. When you stand up for yourself at school, you are learning to have confidence. Don't forget what you have learned!"

"I will always remember. Thank you, Angel!"

Angel smiles and waves at Lydia, then she disappears.

**The End**

# Story Recap

**Problem:** Lydia is being bullied, but she hasn't told any adults. She believes it's her fault, and she no longer wants to attend school.

**Solution:** Angel helps Lydia to recognize that it isn't her fault she is being bullied, and she teaches Lydia to be confident.

**Situation Resolved:** Lydia learns that she is valuable, and that she has many gifts, talents, and abilities. This confidence helps her stand up to the bullies. Lydia also teaches the bullies a lesson: fighting is not the only way, and she doesn't have to say or do anything hurtful to overcome them. In time, Lydia's chant helps other students who are being bullied, and they become Lydia's friends.

**Bullying another child is not cool or fun.**

**Don't be a bully, be a blessing!**

# Questions to Discuss

**What should you do if someone is bullying you?**

1.)   Tell your parents

2.)   Tell your teacher

3.)   If they do not listen, keep telling them!

**What's the best way to stop a bully?**

Self-confidence! Believe in yourself and stand up to the bully.

# Bullying, Not Bullying, or Blessing?
## Please fill in the blanks

1.     Marsha is new to the neighborhood. Pamela shows her around the school and helps her feel comfortable.

_____

2.     Benny and his friends take Mike's lunch money every day.

_____

3.     Franklin hides behind the garage with his water gun. When his sister rides by on her bike, he squirts her in the face. She laughs and rides away.

_____

4.     Kathy got new braces on her teeth. Every day, Robert calls her "brace face."

_____

Answer key: 1. Blessing   2. Bullying   3. Not bullying   4. Bullying

# Please fill in the blanks:

Write about one talent or gift you have.

_____

_____

_____

Write about one thing you love about yourself.

_____

_____

_____

What do you want to be when you grow up?  Why?

_____

_____

_____

_____

## Lydia's Chant
### Practice this chant with your name!

My name is

_____

and I'm the best!

My name is

_____

and I am blessed!

My name is

_____

and I love myself!

www.ingramcontent.com/pod-product-compliance
Lightning Source LLC
Chambersburg PA
CBHW041541240626
47164CB00002B/88